CLAPPER STICK CONCERT

By JohnTom Knight

A Random House PICTUREBACK® Book

Random House 🏠 New York

© 2023 Netflix, Inc. All rights reserved. Published in the United States by Random House Children's Books, a division of Penguin Random House LLC, 1745 Broadway, New York, NY 10019, and in Canada by Penguin Random House Canada Limited, Toronto. SPIRIT RANGERS TM/© Netflix. Used with permission. Pictureback, Random House, and the Random House colophon are registered trademarks of Penguin Random House LLC.

rhcbooks.com

ISBN 978-0-593-57101-9 (trade) — ISBN 978-0-593-64575-8 (ebook)

Printed in the United States of America

10 9 8 7 6 5 4 3 2 1

Photo courtesy of the Samala Chumash

Washington

Oregon

California

SAMALA CHUMASH

THE SAMALA CHUMASH

Spirit Rangers is inspired by the Santa Ynez Band of Chumash Indians, a federally recognized Native American tribe. Xus National Park is based in part on the creeks, forests, wildflowers, and mountains of the tribe's ancestral lands. *Xus* means "bear" in the Samala Chumash language. Many of the characters in this series are inspired by the stories of Samala Chumash matriarch Maria Solares.

The Santa Ynez Band of Chumash Indians is a self-governing sovereign nation and maintains economic self-sufficiency through business development, investments, and the Chumash Casino Resort. The word *Chumash* means "bead money people," and the tribe was known for its sophisticated trading system, made possible by plank canoes, or tomol. A maritime people, the Chumash thrived as boat makers, basket weavers, rock artists, fishermen, and astronomers.

Today the Chumash offer a variety of cultural enrichment programs that maintain and advance the culture and Samala language. Chumash pride and identity is visible through classes and annual events, such as the Chumash Inter-Tribal Pow-Wow, Chumash Culture Day, and Camp Kalawashaq for Chumash youth. Through these ongoing programs and cultural sharing, the Chumash are dedicated to preserving the lands, language, culture, and people.

ourtesy of the Cowlitz Indian Tribe

THE COWLITZ INDIAN TRIBE

The Cowlitz Indian Tribe is a federally recognized Native American tribe located in the Pacific Northwest. Following its recognition in 2000, the tribe focused on business development and has a major casino-resort on its reservation in Ridgefield, Washington, which is of major economic benefit to surrounding counties. Documents from the 1800s describe Cowlitz territory as a placement of four stronghold areas representing cultures suited to mountains, prairies, and lowland rivers. The Cowlitz people were cedar and salmon people, harvesting many species of fish from river systems, as well as wild prairie vegetables and berries from higher elevations. Cowlitz women were famous for their skill in cedar weaving, especially basketry. Cowlitz men were master carvers of cedar and other evergreen and deciduous trees. Their design of the shovel-nosed canoe made them adept at controlling the rivers in a sophisticated trade enterprise. Because their lands contained more prairie than most Salish tribes, the Cowlitz were excellent horse breeders and trainers. The people were multilingual, with the predominant languages being Cowlitz Coast Salish and Sahaptin. Diseases brought by non-native people reduced the population beginning in the 1830s. Today, there are approximately 4,500 enrolled members of the Cowlitz Tribe. The modern Cowlitz Tribe is culturally strong and continues to build its business portfolio. It is also concentrating on bringing the Cowlitz Coast Salish language back after a long dormancy.

It's a warm and sunny day in Xus Park. Junior Park Rangers Kodi, Summer, and Eddy are cleaning up after a birthday party. Summer and Eddy love to play while on the job. They pick up some of the balloons and have a super fun balloon fight!

"Get over here and help me clean before I balloon bop you!" Kodi says to his siblings.

They hear a noise from under the table. *Slurp, slurp, slurp!* Lizard is helping, too!

"Are you eating cake?" asks Eddy, giggling.

"I'm cleaning these plates," says Lizard. "Now let's get to that concert!"

Summer and Eddy are confused. What concert is Lizard talking about?

"The Fish and Otter Spirits have invited us all to play clapper sticks!" Kodi reminds them.

"I love my wansaq'," says Coyote. "*Wansaq*' is the Samala word for clapper stick. *Clappity clap! Clap, clap, clap!*" Coyote does a silly dance on the table with his wansaq'.

Kodi is worried. "We've been so busy with our ranger duties that we haven't made our clapper sticks yet."

"We'll make them in no time," Summer says. "Let's go find DeeDee so she can help us."

The Junior Rangers finish cleaning up and race over to the Visitor Center to see DeeDee. Using wood from an elderberry tree, they carve and sand their own clapper sticks.

"I'm so proud of you!" DeeDee says. "Tribes in California use these instruments for ceremonies or just for fun. You can't rush—"

"Done!" proclaims Summer. She is in such a hurry that she hasn't been listening to DeeDee. Summer's clapper stick still has tree bark and no handle. It doesn't quite look right.

"Can't you go any faster?" Summer asks her brothers. Kodi and Eddy are making their clapper sticks just like DeeDee has shown them.

Soon, Kodi and Eddy finish, and the siblings leave the Visitor Center.
"Does everyone have their clapper stick now?" asks Eddy.
"Yeah, I finished mine *forever* ago," Summer brags.
"Then let's go to Spirit Park!" says Kodi.

The Rangers transform into their Spirit forms! Kodi becomes
Kodi Cub, Summer turns into Summer Hawk, and Eddy poofs
into Eddy Turtle. They're Spirit Ranger ready!

The rangers arrive in Spirit Park just in time. The Fish and Otter Spirits are starting the concert!

The spirits sing in Samala, and the rangers pull out their new clapper sticks to join in, when all of a sudden . . .

"I LIKE MUSIC! I WANT ALL THE MUSIC!" a voice booms. A giant
river monster jumps out of the lake and swallows the whole concert!
 The musicians are trapped in the creature's tummy. The massive fish dives
deep underwater and swims away just as quickly as he arrived.

The Spirit Rangers are shocked!

"What just happened?" Kodi asks.

"We call him Qamash! He's a giant river-swallowing monster spoken of by the Cowlitz Tribe," explains Coyote. "His Cowlitz name is Pasi.k' Ukla'."

"He swallows things he likes and traps them in his see-through belly," adds Lizard.

The Spirit Rangers will save the trapped spirits and the concert!
Eddy blows bubble helmets for everyone so the rangers and their
friends can breathe underwater. Together, the group dives into the
lake to search for Qamash.

The Spirit Rangers search every crook and cranny in the lake. They discover curious water spirits, but Qamash is nowhere to be found!

The group swims back to shore. They need a new plan. "Music always helps me think," says Eddy.

The rangers and their friends take out their clapper sticks and play music together. But Summer's clapper stick breaks! She didn't make it the right way, like Kodi and Eddy did.

FWOOSH! The music from the clapper sticks makes Qamash appear!
"I WANT ALL THE MUSIC RIGHT NOW!" he shouts.

Oh no! Before the Spirit Rangers can say a word to Qamash, he
takes a deep breath and swallows Kodi, Eddy, Coyote, and even Lizard!
Only Summer gets away.

All alone, Summer thinks about what she can do to save her friends. "Qamash likes music . . . but I can't play anything with my broken clapper stick," she says to herself. "I need to go back and ask DeeDee to help me make another!" Summer hurries to Xus Park.

Back at the Visitor Center, Summer rushes in. "DeeDee, I need a new clapper stick right now now now!" she begs.

"Trust me," replies DeeDee. "The slow way is the fast way."

DeeDee carefully shows Summer how to make her clapper stick the right way.

Summer flies back to the lake in Spirit Park with her brand-new clapper stick. She clap-clap-clappity-claps her wansaq'.

"I want all the music **NOW**!" booms Qamash as he leaps out of the lake. He tries to swallow Summer with one big chomp, but she zips out of the way just in time!

"'Now now now' isn't always the right way," Summer tells Qamash. "Sometimes you have to slow things down."

And for the first time, Qamash slows down and listens.

"You're not going to hear music with all the musicians in your belly," Summer says. "You should let them out to play, and then you can hear all the music you like."

"Oh yes!" Qamash shouts excitedly. "Fishy joy!"

Pffft! Qamash spits out Kodi, Eddy, Coyote, Lizard, and all the Otter and Fish Spirits!

"I don't think I'll ever get used to monster slime," says Kodi as he wipes down his fur.

"Way to go, Summer. You saved us!" Eddy cheers.

The show can go on!

"You ready, Otters? You ready, Fishies?" Summer asks. "Hit it!"
The rangers, their friends, and Qamash play beautiful music
together. Everyone has a great time and enjoys the concert.
The Spirit Rangers have saved the day again!